SATISFACTION
GUARANTEED
OR YOUR
MONEY BACK!

To my amiga, Ximena Garcia
Schneider, and to my esposo,
Jay M. Harris. —T.H.

To Mateo and Ines —C.R.

Millbrook Press
A division of Lerner Publishing Group, Inc.
241 First Avenue North
Minneapolis, MN 55401 U.S.A.

Website address: www.lernerbooks.com

Main body text set in Slappy Inline 15/24.
Typeface provided by T26.

Library of Congress Cataloging-in-Publication Data

Harris, Trudy, 1949–
    Say something, Perico / by Trudy Harris ; illustrated by Cecilia Rébora.
        p.   cm.
    Summary: Perico is a Spanish-speaking parrot who lives in a pet store,
and although he works very hard to earn a new home, buyers keep
returning him until the bird, now bilingual, finds the perfect owner. Includes
Spanish glossary and pronunciation guide.
    ISBN: 978–0–7613–5231–0 (lib. bdg. : alk. paper)
    [1. Parrots—Fiction. 2. Pet stores—Fiction. 3. Spanish language—Fiction.
4. Bilingualism—Fiction.] I. Rébora, Cecilia, ill. II. Title.
PZ7.H2439Say 2011
[E]—dc22   2011001114

Manufactured in the United States of America
1 – BC – 7/15/11

Say Something, Perico

Trudy Harris

illustrated by
Cecilia Rébora

M Millbrook Press • Minneapolis

A woman wearing purple glasses peered into Perico's cage. "Does this bird talk?" she asked.

"Well," said the pet store man, "he can say *some* words."

The woman pointed at Perico. "Say something, bird. Say, 'Polly wants a cracker.'" She spoke louder. "Say, 'POLLY—WANTS—A—CRACKER.'"

Perico looked at the woman. He opened his beak, but the only sound to come out was a screechy,

"P-p-p-paaaaK."

The woman laughed. "Goofy bird," she said, "can't even say 'Polly wants a cracker.'"

Perico's wings drooped. He scooted behind his empty water dish. As the woman turned to go, Perico opened his beak again.

"Agua!" he squawked.

"Wait! He's talking," said the pet store man.

"Agua," Perico called, "agua, agua!"

"What is he saying?" the woman asked.

"I think he's trying to say *opera*," the store man said. "Maybe he wants to go to the opera."

"A bird that enjoys opera? I enjoy the opera!" said the woman. "I could take him with me tonight."

"Just give it a try," said the store man. "If it doesn't work out, you can bring him back tomorrow."

At the opera, Perico perched on the woman's hat. Performers strutted and sang onstage. Then,

"Aaaaaaaa

"aawk!"

Perico let out a long, piercing note. It was higher than even the soprano could sing.

"What's that horrible noise?" a man gasped.

"Stop that awful squawking!" a woman snapped.

The woman with the purple glasses stood up and hurried out the door.

The next morning, the woman brought Perico back to the pet store. "I should have bought a gerbil!" she said with a huff. "At least gerbils are quiet."

The store man looked at Perico. "If you want a new home," he said, "you're going to have to quit screeching and learn to say, 'Polly wants a cracker.'"

So that night, after all the other animals had fallen asleep, Perico whispered to himself. He practiced over and over. By morning, Perico could say, "Polly wants a cracker."

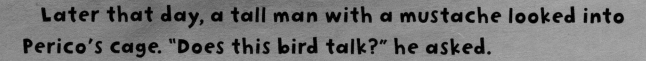

Later that day, a tall man with a mustache looked into Perico's cage. "Does this bird talk?" he asked.

"Well," said the pet store man, "he can say *some* words."

"How are you, bird?" the tall man asked. Can you say, 'I am fine today'?" The man spoke louder, "Say, 'I—AM—FINE—TODAY.'"

This time, Perico didn't screech. He made no sound at all.

"Dumb bird," the tall man said, "can't even say, 'I am fine today.'"

"He said something yesterday," the pet store man replied.

The tall man leaned so close that his mustache poked between the wires of Perico's cage. "Dumb bird, HOW—ARE—YOU?"

Perico lowered his head.

"Mal," he answered quietly.

"Wait! He's talking," the pet store man said. "I think he wants to go to the mall."

"A bird that likes shopping? I like to shop!" said the tall man. "We could go to the mall together!"

"Just give it a try," the pet store man said. "If it doesn't work out, you can bring him back tomorrow."

In the mall, Perico rode quietly on the tall man's shoulder until they came to some trees. Perico stretched his wings and flew to the treetops. Then he glided by large men's clothing, swooped above ladies' coats, and darted into children's shoes.

"There's a birdie in the store!" a little girl squealed.

"Stop that parrot!" a clerk shrieked.

Perico landed on the tall man's shoulder. The man frowned until his mustache turned upside down.

The tall man stomped back to the pet store. "I should have bought a boa," he said with a scowl. "At least snakes don't fly."

The store man shrugged. "If you want a new home," he said to Perico, "you're going to have to quit flapping about and learn to say, 'I am fine today.'"

So Perico practiced—almost all night.
At last, he could say, "I am fine today."

The next day, a man with no hair stopped near Perico's cage. "Does this bird talk?" he asked.

"Well," said the pet store man, "he can say *some* words."

The bald man squinted at Perico. "Say, 'I am a pretty bird.'" He spoke louder, "Say, 'I—AM—A—PRETTY—BIRD.'"

Perico stayed silent.

"Silly parrot," the man said, "can't even say, 'I am a pretty bird.'"

The pet store man looked at Perico. "Don't you want a new home—a real home?" he asked.

Perico's head bobbed up and down.

"Sí,"
Perico answered.

"Wait! He's talking," the pet store man said. "I think he wants to go to the sea."

"A bird that loves the sea? I love the sea!" said the bald man. "I could take him on my boat."

"Just give it a try," the store man said. "If it doesn't work out, you can bring him back tomorrow."

On the boat, Perico didn't sing. He didn't fly. Instead, he watched playful swimming fish. They turned, swished their tails, and turned again. Perico turned and swished too. In dizzy circles, he spun around and around until he tumbled . . . tailfirst into the water.

"Bird overboard!" the bald man yelled.
"Grab him with the net!" another man shouted.

23

Faster than feathers dry, the bald man marched
Perico back to the pet store. "I should have bought
a turtle!" the bald man said with a snort. "At least
a turtle could swim."

The pet store man rubbed his head. "If you want a
new home," he said, "you're going to have to behave
yourself and learn to say, 'I am a pretty bird.'"

So that night, Perico practiced.

The next day, a young boy with a
cheery smile skipped toward Perico's
cage. Perico smoothed his feathers
and sat up tall. But the boy passed by
without giving Perico a glance.

"Polly wants a cracker," Perico squawked.

The boy paid no attention to Perico. Instead, he walked toward a spinning gerbil.

"I am fine today," Perico called.

The boy turned to look at a sleeping snake.

"I am a pretty bird," Perico tried again. He tried louder. "I—AM—A—PRETTY—BIRD."

This time, the boy gently tapped a glass box where a striped turtle swam. The boy nodded as his mother opened her purse.

Perico hung his head.

The boy whirled around. "That bird speaks both English and Spanish," he said. "I speak English and Spanish! This parrot could be the perfect pet."

Perico flapped his wings and sat straighter than ever.

"Yo soy un pájaro bonito!" he squawked.

"Clever bird," the mother said.

"Can we take him home?" the boy asked. "Please, please, por favor."

The mother looked at Perico. Then she smiled at her son and answered, "Sí."

"Remember, young man," the store man said, "if it doesn't work out, you can bring the bird back tomorrow."

But Perico never came back.

Study this word list and practice like Perico did. You'll soon be saying lots of words in both English and Español.

agua (AH-gwah): **water**

bien (bee-EHN): **fine, good**

bonito (or bonita) (boh-NEE-toh/boh-NEE-tah): **pretty**

casa (KAH-sah): **house, home**

Español (eh-spahn-YOHL): **Spanish**

estoy (eh-STOY): **am, I'm**

galleta (gah-YAY-tah): **cracker, cookie**

hoy (OY): **today**

mal (MAHL): **bad, badly**

mi (MEE): **my**

no (NOH): **no**

pájaro (PAH-hah-roh): **bird**

para (PAH-rah): **for**

perico (peh-REE-koh): **a parrot or a talkative person**

por favor (POR fah-VOR): **please**

quiere (kee-EH-ray): **wants**

sí (SEE): **yes**

soy (SOY): **am, I'm**

un (OON): **a**

una (OON-ah): **a**

yo (YOH): **I**

Can you read these sentences?

Perico quiere una galleta.

Estoy bien hoy.

Yo soy un pájaro bonito.

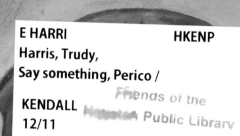